Morning Glories

Shawn Tinsley

Order this book online at www.trafford.com/08-0978
or email orders@trafford.com

Most Trafford titles are also available at major online book retailers.

Note for Librarians: A cataloguing record for this book is available from Library and Archives Canada at www.collectionscanada.ca/amicus/index-e.html

ISBN: 978-1-4251-8451-3

We at Trafford believe that it is the responsibility of us all, as both individuals and corporations, to make choices that are environmentally and socially sound. You, in turn, are supporting this responsible conduct each time you purchase a Trafford book, or make use of our publishing services. To find out how you are helping, please visit www.trafford.com/responsiblepublishing.html

Our mission is to efficiently provide the world's finest, most comprehensive book publishing service, enabling every author to experience success. To find out how to publish your book, your way, and have it available worldwide, visit us online at www.trafford.com/10510

www.trafford.com

North America & international
toll-free: 1 888 232 4444 (USA & Canada)
phone: 250 383 6864 • fax: 250 383 6804 • email: info@trafford.com

The United Kingdom & Europe
phone: +44 (0)1865 487 395 • local rate: 0845 230 9601
facsimile: +44 (0)1865 481 507 • email: info.uk@trafford.com

10 9 8 7 6 5 4 3

THE BIBLE IS God's spoken word of love to us. I pray that the love of God is revealed to you as you read and study his ways and will for your life. I pray that this book will inspire you to see the love that God has for you and the victory he has already won for you. May you be truly blessed and feel truly loved-because you are! More than you will ever know!

I GIVE THANKS to God for blessing me with a gift and passion for writing and for my husband who gave me continual encouragement while writing this book.

How to use this Book

THIS BOOK IS intended to encourage you to see scripture and Jesus in a new light. Each story is meant to show how a daily walk with Jesus can enrich our lives and the lives of others. At the end of each story are Journaling Pages listing the individual scriptures that were found throughout the previous story. Space is provided after each scripture passage for writing down what the Holy Spirit reveals to you during your study. There is also room for additional notes for more in depth study as the Spirit leads you.

Table of Contents

1

That's my girl!

RUBEN FRANK ROSE this morning, as he does every morning, to the sound of rustling bed covers, running water and squeaking wheelchairs. All courtesy of the nursing staff who come in to wake his dear bride of more than 50 years to bath, dress and ready her for the day. This was the daily routine before breakfast was served in the main dining hall of the assisted living community in which they now live.

During this time, as well as throughout the day, he sits in his recliner by the window. The blinds are positioned at just the right angle to allow perfect sight of any passersby in the corridor at the other end of the garden atrium, adjacent to his only remaining physical view of the world.

This was his "space", an area large enough only to fit a chair, table and lamp. A place he seemed to have carved out for himself that somehow connected him to the outside world, if only by a window. Although this window seat had become a treasured possession, it was hardly a rivaled comparison to his Florida home of ample room, rich land and plentiful rivers which seem to sing a song of solace as their waters rush over the rocky banks.

As his nurse, I was able to talk with him on a regular basis during our weekly visits. Yet, as we chatted and I listened to him tell his stories of the life he lived, I began to realize that this small window view that he was so protective of was more than a connection to the outdoors. It was the last remaining vehicle he possessed in retrieving the precious memories of his past; his hobbies, his passions, his achievements and failures, his "pride-and-joy" moments and of course, his loves.

He spoke of younger days living in Florida on the river as the party boats sailed by with their music flowing upstream to fill the air that pour into his bedroom window at night. He also told with pride how he became a prominent pilot and expert welder as a young man trying to make his way. Each rendition shared revealed only a small section of his life, yet gave a little more insight to the man he was and the life he relished so. The most poignant were the stories of how he first met his sweet bride who doesn't talk much these days and requires constant care and assistance for the simplest of tasks regarding her own personal care.

Even though she could give little if any response as he spoke, he would give her a glance and a pat on the hand as he said, "That's my girl!" Many of his stories would be followed by the phrase, "I miss my home. Florida-that's my home. This isn't home for me but I'm here because she needs to be here and that's my girl".

Then immediately, the story of how they met would come to his mind and he recounted the events as if for the first time, with a slight grin and a look in his eyes of wonder as to how something so incredible could have happened to him. He-the young, handsome military pilot and her-the beautiful student who fell in love almost immediately and have been together ever since.

They shared a life of more that fifty years full of rough beginnings, triumphs, losses, children and grandchildren. Upon first glance, evidence of the fullness of their life consisted of only a handful of family photos; the usual holiday snapshots of the "kids" with their "kids". Three generations represented in a handful of pictures displayed in a room for two, which was no bigger than a walk-in closet. A closet they now called home.

One photo stood out among the rest. The one Ruben referred

to frequently with great pride and a huge smile was that of his 'girl' the day they met. Of all his stories, he admitted, "She's the best thing to happen in my life". Many of the stories he told were the same ones he had told before. As I listened, I found myself wondering if his memory was really failing him to the extent of repeating his stories or was there more. Maybe, he was aware of his repetitive nature more than I realized. Maybe the comfort found in repeating those memories was worth the possible diagnosis of dementia he might have received.

The list of things we do for love is endless. They can take us away from the home and life we've always known. As Ruben put it, "I want to go back home. I can't because she needs to be here where she can be taken care of. She's here therefore I'm here. Where else would I be? That's my girl!"

THE TRUE LOVE and devotion of a Godly marriage is a perfect example of God's love for his people. Listed below are scripture references, which describe these relationships and correlations of their characteristics to each other.

Eph. 4:2-6 ______________________________

____

____

____

____

____

Eph. 5:21-30 ______________________________

____

____

____

____

____

Col. 3:18-19 ______________________________

____

____

____

____

____

1 Peter 3:7 ______________________________

____

____

____

____

2

The Curtain

WHAT DO YOU do when you know a friend is hurting? You hurt too, don't you? You also want to do whatever you can to ease the hurt; to help them through that difficult time. We've all been in that type of situation more than once yet at times it is still tough to know the right thing to do. I recall one particular occasion when I faced just such a dilemma. The answer I was given caught me blind sighted and changed both our lives.

My friend had a deep heartache that she tried to hide. I knew something was wrong but was unsure what it was or how I could help. One night as we were talking, she finally opened up to me and told me that of all the struggles she faced or losses she had endured, the most hurtful one was the lost relationship between her and Jesus. She told me of how close she used to be and how she would worship and study the Bible but because of past mistakes she didn't feel she could do either, which caused her to feel very distant. As I listened, my mind raced to find the right words to say that would comfort her and give her the answer she needed. I told her that God loved her and would always want a relationship with her but as I spoke I realized I was saying things that I hadn't spoken of or even allowed myself to think of in quite a while. Feeling as if I were loosing this battle to help my friend, I instinctively did something I hadn't done in a long time. I prayed! I said, "Lord, what can I do to help her be close to you again?" I immediately heard, "How can you help her be close to me when you're not close to me?" Talk about something that gets your attention! That was truth hitting me square in the face!

At that moment, in my mind's eye, I saw a curtain being pulled back to reveal all the things that I allowed myself to participate in that was not pleasing to God. Things in my life that pulled me away from him and things that took my time and focus prohibiting me from hearing his voice were all set center stage for me to acknowledge as that curtain was raised. Like one of the final acts of a dark Elizabethan play, my life as I was living it was in plain view for me to see as God saw it. In that moment, God allowed me to feel a fraction of the sorrow he felt as he watched me pursue this life of sin, emptiness and distance from him. As tears streamed down my face, I prayed to God that he would forgive me for the way I was living and for neglecting my own relationship with him. I asked him to teach me how to draw close and stay close to him. At that very moment, I felt a flood of warmth, love and acceptance. Although at the time I did not know the verse, I experienced the evidence of Psalm 145:18-19 that says, "The Lord is near all who call on him, to all who call on him in truth. He fulfills the desires of those who fear him; he hears their cry and saves them". I knew that God had heard my prayer. All this happened in a matter of mere seconds and was unknown to my friend on the other end of the line-but I knew it! My heart was alive again and on fire! The words I struggled to find to help my friend were now being given to me by my loving Father!

I will never forget that day. The day God reached me through helping a friend. James 4:8 of the Bible says, "Come near to God and he will come near to you". As I continued to seek out knowledge of him, I felt strengthened and secure as he revealed his promises to me. He's still filling me with his strength by blessing me with knowledge of him. This knowledge guides me and gives council to family, friends and those whom God brings into my path. Throughout the Bible we can read of the mercy of the Lord to not hold our failures against us if we give them over to him. God is called compassion's Father and the "God of all comfort, who comforts us in all our troubles, so we can comfort those in any trouble with the comfort we ourselves have received from God" (2 Cor. 1:4). I lived that verse long before I knew it. He used the troubles of a friend to get my attention and bring me close to him. Then he turned it around by providing me the words needed to reach and comfort my friend.

It's amazing how God can reach the most obscure regions, the dark and hidden parts of our hearts, with something as small and seemingly insignificant as a word or two. Especially when you think you've successfully placed all those 'dark spots' out of sight behind a curtain. The mercy of God is gentle enough to wrap you in love yet sharp enough to pierce your heart with the stinging truth that's needed to change your life for the better.

I may never have fifteen minutes of fame, my name in lights or be center stage on Broadway but God gave me my 'curtain call'- I'm so glad he did!

Psalm 145:18-19 ______________________________

James 4:8 ______________________________

2 Corinthians 1:4 ______________________________

ADDITIONAL NOTES

3

Parents Dream

HAVE YOU EVER woken up after having a strange dream and thought, "Wow, that pizza I ate last night must not have agreed with me." Or maybe, "I shouldn't have watched that movie just before going to bed." What about a daydream when you are fully awake? A mental picture that seems so real yet you know that it's only in your mind. One that is different from the usual ones of wishing you were on the beach instead of at work or that you could strike oil in your back yard, become a millionaire and retire permanently! One that is seemingly out of the blue and can't be attributed to any logical influences such as over indulging in a tub of rocky road ice cream! What then would cause such visualizations and what if any meaning could they have? One day in my early adulthood, I remember experiencing just such an occasion. The only way I could describe it was that it was a vision from God. At the time, I never would have imagined that it would take me nearly 15 years to realize the true meaning of that vision, what God was trying to tell me and for what he was trying to prepare me.

You are probably wondering right now what could possibly be so life defining about a simple 'daydream'? Well, I'll tell you. When it comes from God you know it and you also know that he definitely has a very good reason for it! So now you're probably asking, "What was this epic mental image?" To which I say, "I'm glad you asked". It all started with seeing myself standing in the middle of an open field and being surrounded by many children of all sizes, ages, colors and nationalities running, playing and laughing around me. As I stood and watched this heartwarming scene I heard a voice say, "You are responsible for all these but none belong to you". After I got over the initial shock of this image I began to contemplate its meaning. I eventually resolved to view it as a sign that I would one day work in international mission work with children, probably medical.

As the years went by I held tight to that message I received from the Lord and knew one day he would make a clear way for my mission work. Meanwhile, I ran into a friend I hadn't seen in years and felt an immediate burden for her. A few days later we spoke on the phone and she opened her heart to me of some very weighted issues she was facing. Over the next three months we continued to talk and I counseled her, telling her what God says in his word about her situation. Several months later I saw her out and I noticed a light in her eyes that was previously missing as she said with a big smile, "The situation I was in before is over and my life is better now." I knew there had been a major change in her life. Within a couple of months another person crossed my path that I felt drawn to and began to talk with about struggles she was going through. I began to see a pattern developing. God would bring one person after another into my life for a specific reason. He would put a burden on my heart and give me words to counsel and sometimes even a prophetic word of guidance. As I began to notice this pattern, I felt very inadequate for such a task and very unsure that my assessment of this pattern was even correct. The only thing I knew to do was to talk to a dear friend who I knew to be a very strong and wise woman of God. As I spoke I began to tell her the burdens on my heart and the pattern as it appeared to me. Not knowing exactly how to explain to her what I really didn't understand myself, she gently smiled and said, "You have just found your purpose. This is the purpose God has for your life. You find hurting people, help and counsel them". Years later I learned the term for this ministry is known as "spiritual parenting". One of the first references in the New Testament that explains this concept is in 1 Corinthians 4:9 as Paul spoke of Timothy as his 'son' and how he would remind the Corinthians the principles of Christ as he learned them from Paul. Then, the scriptures reveal how Paul describes Timothy like "a son with his father" when he spoke of how Timothy took what he learned from him to teach others (Phil 2:22).

God's word tells us to be ever conscious of the things we say and how they affect others. God calls us to speak only what will "build others up according to their needs, that it may benefit those who listen" (Eph 4:29). In addition to this, it also says in 2 Timothy 2:2 that things spoken in accordance with God's word be "entrusted to reliable men who will also be qualified to teach others".

Each of these scriptures focus on how the Lord wants us to learn and draw near to him, then use our God given knowledge to help others draw close to him. God doesn't have to have our help to make Himself known. He is God and can reveal himself directly to people in any way he chooses. However, he chose to design his work and revelation through the sharing of believers. Beyond giving him praise for his comfort, compassion, grace and knowledge of him, we are to share these things with others. In doing so we honor God, strengthen our relationship with him and edify others at the same time.

God has led me to learn many things, most of which is that I have much to learn! He has also brought many beautiful people into my life, even if for just a short time, and blessed me with the privilege of being used by him to help them draw closer to him. It is an awesome experience to have a front row seat to see God break the chains of bondage, oppression and sin off of someone's life! Sitting in that seat is an honor and a very humbling place to be. To see God's amazing grace in action and to be able to help others realize that the Lord is ready and waiting to give them more than enough grace to free them from anything and everything that is holding them down is awesome! Parents always want the best for their children and strive to teach them and provide for them everything necessary to achieve happiness and success. How much more does God want that for his children? Oh, to be one of his agents to proclaim the way to true life, liberty and freedom.

How could I ever realize at 20 years old that a simple 'daydream' could mean so much? Thanks to the Lord that loved me so much as to bless me with such a gift-to be used by him! Don't ever dismiss the seemingly insignificant because it just could be God calling you to an amazing ministry and a ringside seat to his glory!

1 Corinthians 4:9 ______________________________

Philippians 2:22 ______________________________

Ephesians 4:29 ______________________________

2 Timothy 2:2 ______________________________

ADDITIONAL NOTES

4

Consider the Cost

A MOTHER PLANNING dinner for her family while trying to maintain the household budget considers the cost of the ingredients of the meal she plans. A carpenter carefully measures and plans for the necessary supplies he needs before building a house to manage the cost. Every decision that is made must be compared to the alternative and the cost of its consequences. A wise man considers the cost in all things; not just for the present but also the future. How foolish a man would be to think himself wise to view the possessions he can see but yet give no consideration to the neglect of his soul.

If in the drive to gain in the here-and-now, we neglect the growth and life of our soul, which is the part that longs for God, then we have gained nothing. Earthly wealth whether monetary or as the pursuit for personal gratification, will eventually turn to dust. Eternity is a long time to carry around pockets full of dust! The most profitable of investors goes to an expert in the area that he wishes to invest. Doesn't it make sense to consult the 'Wonderful Counselor' for the most important investment of our lives? The Bible says, "Seek ye first the kingdom of God and all these things will be added to you." No bank in the world can ever yield a better return than that! To invest in Christ means to give up your own control and to give up self; self-promotion, self-centeredness, self-preservation, self-sufficiency, self-loathing, self-doubt, self-self. It is a choice. You can choose not to sacrifice self but everyone will sacrifice something, if not self than soul. It can't work both ways no matter what the devil tries to make you believe. You can't have it all unless you give it all. Give all of yourself to him. Give all your guilt, shame, pride, superiority, fear, worry, doubt, jealously, pettiness, control or any other controlling substance in your life.

Lose control to gain freedom, it's worth the cost!

JOURNALING PAGE

5

Eyes of Love

ONE DAY AT work I came across a coworker who was going through a difficult time in her life and appeared to be very sad, quite, preoccupied and withdrawn. Her eyes were downcast and seemed to be void of light. Though she didn't speak much, she communicated volumes to reflect her mood and emotions. I couldn't help but notice that her eyes could not contain the message, which she refused to speak with her mouth. This experience reminded me of a proverb about how the eyes are the windows of the soul. I began to think of the truth in that statement and how much is revealed of a person through the eyes. The Bible says that the eye is the light of the body (Luke 11:34). This can explain how we are able to share our feelings or possibly even our personal convictions without speaking a word. Sadness, pain, joy, fear, anger, love and hatred as well as many other emotions or even ones mental state can be seen through the eyes of that person. This shows how the mind and body affect each other and how hiding ones true feelings or even personal character may prove difficult at times.

Have you ever spoken with someone who had expressive eyes? As they recalled a story, did their eyes seem to accentuate the very point being made by the verbal communication given? Imagine living during Jesus time on earth as one of his disciples, privileged to personally observe him speaking, teaching, and healing. What message would his eyes portray to you? Envision being able to have a conversation with him as the disciples did. Would you see passion in his eyes to strengthen the reality of his message and give insight to its true meaning of power and potential to change lives? I think you would. The Bible continually speaks of the love of Christ. The book of John is considered the book of love because it describes the love Jesus had for all mankind. How can a heart so full of love and compassion refrain from flooding the eyes with a reflection of the same? To see the expressive eyes of Jesus, you merely have to choose one of the many compassionate stories in the Bible and step into the shoes of the main character. Take, for instance, the story of the widow's only son. When Jesus saw the widow in pain, he had compassion on her and told her not to cry. Because he had love for her and felt her sorrow, he touched her son's coffin and gave the command that brought him back to life (Luke 7:13-15). Imagine being that mother looking into the eyes of the one who gave you the gift of your son-alive! Another report tells how he responded when confronted with the death of Lazarus. Jesus saw his sister weeping, was troubled in spirit and wept also as he called Lazarus to come forth-raising him from the dead (John 11: 32-44). How his eyes must have danced with joy to be able to give such restoration to these people whom he loved so much. He was fully committed to sharing in the lives of those around him and openly expressed his love and compassion for them.

His entire earthly existence was dedicated to love, life and giving both to others. How could anyone ever find any wrong in that? The religion scholars did and wanted him stopped at any cost. They decided that the only price sufficient was to forever extinguish the eyes that sparked life to the hopeless and shed light in dark places. The eyes and life of Jesus became the payment they required (John 19:7). The life that lived for others and began on earth for the purpose of bringing hope to the world was not welcomed and suffered for it. The suffering was brutal and did not only encompass physical beating but scorning, ridicule and persecution from Roman soldiers (Luke 22:63-67). While enduring this torture, he also faced abandonment of those he considered to be his closest companions-the result was isolation and loneliness. During each ordeal he presented love and compassion that, I believe, could not be contained by his eyes. This expression of intense love for us and for God's will was evident in his eyes even though his flesh caused him to feel every hurt just as deeply as any one of us would. How do I know? The Bible states that when Jesus was taken to the high priest's house, Peter (one of the twelve disciples) being close enough to see him, denied Jesus to the crowd outside. Immediately, Peter was convicted with one look from the loving eyes of Jesus and he began to sob from the grief of his betrayal (Luke 22:54-62).

During the arrest and trial of Jesus, the ones who received the benefit of his love the most were the same ones who were demanding his crucifixion while the soldiers took joy in mocking and beating him (Luke 23:23). Throughout it all he never spoke a word in retaliation and continued to regard them with love. This love was apparent even amid the excruciating pain of hanging on a cross by nails driven through the hands and feet. First, when Jesus gazed down at his mother with eyes of compassion as he said to his disciple John to care for her as his own (John 19:26-27). Then, as he saw past his own suffering and considered with mercy the ones directly responsible for his anguish as he prayed on their behalf for God's forgiveness (Luke 24:34). It seems that anyone would find it nearly impossible to even imagine looking at someone who caused so much misery with love or mercy-but Jesus did. Love continued to radiate from his presence when he turned eyes full of grace to the thief on the cross next to him as he reassured the man of his eternity (Luke 24:39-43).

He still restores us today with mercy and grace that flows through eyes of love, which he reveals to all who have the desire to know him. He blesses that desire with the ability to envision his eyes covered in blood and swollen but full of love as he hung on the cross for the very ones that put him there-all of humanity. The eyes that wept with compassion, convicted with truth, healed with grace and renewed with hope; those eyes can do the same today if we permit ourselves to be drawn as so many were all those years ago. So allow yourself to be drawn to the eyes of hope, truth, grace and mercy-the eyes of love.

Luke 11:34 ____

____

____

____

____

Luke 7:13-15____

____

____

____

____

John 11: 32-44 ____________________________________

____

____

____

____

John 19:7____

____

____

____

____

Luke 22:63-67 ____________________________________

____

____

____

____

Luke 22:54-62

Luke 23:23

John 19:26-27

Luke 24:34

Luke 24:39-43

ADDITIONAL NOTES

6

To Be Like John

RECENTLY I READ a passage of scripture during my devotional time that brought tears to my eyes and humbled my heart. I had heard this story before as well as read it for myself. However, this particular time the words seemed to jump off the page and drag me by the collar into the scene to witness it for myself. What I saw changed me, changed my heart and created a desire for a deeper relationship with Jesus.

The particular verse is part of the account of the last supper when Jesus washed the disciples feet. He realized that the twelve were hesitant and didn't understand why it was necessary that he wash their feet so, before he began he said, "If I do not wash you, you have no part in me. He who is bathed need only to wash his feet but is completely clean, but not all of you are clean (John13:8-10)". He took care in clarifying that he knew there was a betrayer among them when he affirmed that not all were clean. Then he explained that as he became a servant to them by washing their feet, they should do likewise for each other serving in the same way. He went on to describe that "a servant is not greater than his master nor is he who is sent greater than the one who sent him (John 13:16)".

As they heard these words they were eager to know whom the guilty one was and urged John to ask Jesus specifically which one of them would betray him. The interesting and even poignant moment that followed is one that seems to define John's relationship to Jesus and spoke to my heart greatly as one that I can use as a life model. This event was when John began to ask his question, he leaned back resting his head against Jesus chest. Did you get that? John, a fallible man with limited understanding who, like you and I, must learn some lessons over and over asking for forgiveness repeatedly. This imperfect man felt so much love, passion and devotion for Jesus while at the same time was completely comfortable in acting upon those profoundly heartfelt feelings by getting as close as possible to the one he loved so much. Image loving so intensely that you can't get enough! Think about having your heart and life touched so deeply and dramatically that you can't resist but to 'touch' back. To touch the Lord may seem like an odd concept to most considering that we are all taught to 'ask and wait for a touch from God'. Did you know that God can be touched? We are made in his image; so if we can be touched, so can he. There is power in reaching out and touching Jesus that can restore, deliver and heal. Just look at the woman with the issue of blood. She tried everything she knew for twelve years but nothing worked. She didn't want to wait any longer. So she fought the crowd, reached out and touched Jesus by the hem of his robe. Instead of passively waiting she actively sought the Lord. I Chronicles 28:9 says, "If you seek him, you will find him." She had an unquenchable desire for Jesus. That was John. He was totally uninhibited in showing his affection and devotion to Jesus, wanting to be as close as possible and never wanting to leave his side. I want to be like John. If I could choose a role model regardless of time frame, I would choose John for his example of giving himself to the Lord without thinking twice.

I truly believe that actions such as those please God. Throughout the Bible scripture reveals how the Lord wants us all to come to him as a child. Jesus says in Matthew 18:3-5, "Except you be converted and become as little children, you shall not enter into the kingdom of heaven. Whosoever shall humble himself as this little child, the same is greatest in the kingdom of heaven and whoever receives one such child in my name receives me." Why would he instruct us to be childlike? Because children love and show love before they think. The love of a child has no ulterior motive or self-serving pretense. This is what the Lord specifies as to what is required to enter his kingdom. He wants all to be with him in eternity which is why I know God smiles when he sees us reach out to him in love, adoration, worship and praise as children who want nothing less than to be in continual contact both physically and emotionally to the one we love so deeply.

There is no better way to honor our Lord. We have nothing to give but what he has already given us so the best offering to present to God is a free showing of our desire for him. By declaring an offering of desire for more of him, he hears our plea and grants our request showering us with love, filling us with his presence, increasing our knowledge of him, directing our path and drawing us ever closer to him.

We are his children and what child doesn't want to make her father proud? God takes pride in us when we are obedient and is glorified when we reach out to him in all aspects of our lives. When we seek him to give praise for the good times as well as to ask for guidance or protection for the difficult ones we are acknowledging him as our sole provider, redeemer and Lord just as John did. John referred to himself as the beloved disciple because of the profoundly loving relationship developed between himself and Jesus-his friend, teacher and Lord.

The more I meditate on that idea, the more I realize that I want to be like John. So relaxed and free in the presence of my Lord that I don't hesitate to rest my head on his chest as I open my heart to him.

John 13:8-10 ______________________________

John 13:16 ______________________________

1 Chronicles 28:9 ______________________________

Matthew 18:3-5 ______________________________

ADDITIONAL NOTES

7

Prayer for a Friend

WEBSTER'S DICTIONARY DEFINES a friend as a person whom one knows well and has strong affection or love for. The Bible says there are three constants: faith, hope and love but the greatest is love. One of God's greatest blessings of love is the gift of friendship-a bond that grows deeper and stronger everyday. This is my prayer to God for his blessing on you-my friend!

Lord I ask you to bless my very special friend

She has a heart of gold and love that never ends

She shows compassion for others with a heart that's good

and true

I pray for love and protection in all that she may do

Lord Bless my Friend

JOURNALING PAGE

8

Directionally Challenged

HAVE YOU NOTICED that in the society of today we have a politically correct title for nearly everything. People no longer have disabilities but challenges. I guess it does sound better and it definitely gives a more positive impression than the former. I am proud to say that I have been blessed with many things but I have to admit that an internal compass is not one of them. When it comes to travel I am disabled-I mean 'directionally challenged'. If my husband and I go on a trip to a place we've never been before he is the one to drive and map out the course because if I did we might end up on a scenic tour to nowhere. Since he is so meticulous in finding the most accurate and direct route possible (and I obviously am not) we get to our destination without a lot of stress and wasted time.

Did you know that God has placed in each of his children an internal compass for their life? No, this compass is not given for the purpose of getting you to that vacation spot in record time and it is not intended to be a homing device when you've made a wrong turn that took you twenty miles in the opposite direction. Although it could do both of these things, it has a much more important purpose in our lives. This 'it' is actually a 'he' and his ultimate goal is to direct each of us along our God given path. He is called the Holy Spirit.

So who is this Holy Spirit you ask? After the resurrection Jesus appeared to the disciples and explained to them that they would receive power and guidance to be his witnesses to all the earth and then he was taken into heaven. In accordance with Jesus previous teaching, during the feast of Pentecost, which was observed to signify the end of the harvest, these followers of Christ had "divided tongues, as of fire, to sit upon them and they were filled with the Holy Spirit causing them to speak in tongues, witness and perform signs and wonder in Christ's name" (Acts chapter 2). The Holy Spirit was sent to be a helper as he led these people in the righteous and prosperous life God planned for them. By the Holy Spirit's revealing power working in them, the deep things of God were made known to them causing them to grow in faith and faithfulness.

Some may ask, "If I have this internal compass then why am I so confused and why does my life seem like such a mess?" As with any gift that a person receives he can choose to leave it in the box and place it on a shelf never to be used or thought of again. Just because we have been given the Holy Spirit that does not mean we can automatically set the cruise control and take a nap until we wake up in that magical place called 'our destiny'. If we do not sincerely ask the Holy Spirit to speak to us and guide us we are not accessing the only reliable source of direction that we have for our lives. After we ask him for guidance we have to be quite enough and still enough to receive the answers he has for us. Following the leading of the Holy Spirit makes the difference between living a life of prosperity as God wants or turmoil as the world provides.

"Those who live by the flesh set their minds on fleshly things which is destructive but those who live by the Spirit set their minds on spiritual things which produces life and peace" (Romans 8:5-11). To have your mind on fleshly things is to live as the world does, which is displeasing to God. If you have the Spirit of God in you, which is the Holy Spirit then you live as though you are dead to the lures of this world that promote a sinful nature. Those who rely on their own understanding don't have the Spirit because the Spirit guides in truth and intercedes for us by praying to God on our behalf for what is best for us. How does he guide? He uses many ways to get our attention such as an inner voice during our quite time or by the timely spoken words of those whom God uses in our lives. The primary way the Spirit speaks to us is when we read the holy scriptures. Ephesians 6:17 says that "the word of God is the sword of the Spirit", which he uses to pierce our hearts with the truth of the Lord as well as equip us with the ultimate weapon to defend ourselves and our faith against the spiritual war we all face in the battles of day-to-day life on earth.

When we learn to listen to the Holy Spirit, he reveals more of Jesus to us and gives strength, power and the ability to better understand the magnitude of Christ's love for us. The disciple Peter provided an ideal example of the benefit of listening to the Holy Spirit. He had a vision of how God wanted him to witness to all people regardless of religion or nationality and because he listen and followed the instruction he was given many nations received the message of Jesus' saving grace (Acts 10:9-28).

The Spirit also gives each of us gifts to edify and help others. Among these gifts are wisdom, knowledge, faith, discernment, prophesy, healing, speaking in tongues and interpretation of tongues (I Cor. 12:7-11). As we use these Spirit given gifts in the way Christ intended we are blessed in our own lives through our submission and obedience to God. Because we are human and live in a sinful world, it is difficult at times to know what God wants for our lives but if we allow ourselves to recognize the guiding voice of the Holy Spirit we can gain understanding of the ways of God and his will for our daily lives as well as our future.

So if there really is such a thing as being directionally challenged (and I am proof there is) it is very reassuring to know I have an unfailing compass that can give my life direction if I merely allow him to speak to me and allow myself to listen.

Acts chapter 2 ______________________________

Romans 8:5-11 ______________________________

Ephesians 6:17 ______________________________

Acts 10:9-28 ______________________________

I Cor. 12:7-11 ______________________________

ADDITIONAL NOTES

9

Detour on Damascus Road

DETOURS CAN BE so annoying. They are almost always unexpected and throw plans off schedule. In fact, I have to deal with one in my own neighborhood. It took several days for me to remember that I couldn't get through the path that I am so use to traveling. A couple of times I forgot and didn't realize the detour until I was already halfway down the road. This caused me to have to retrace my own path back to the main road when I came to the roadblock. This detour was causing a major inconvenience and a lot of stress. The reason for the detour is actually to widen a bridge on the road and not to mess up my day as I have claimed in frustration so many times. So, even though the detour was not part of my plan, it will make life better in the long run.

Most detours are the same way; such a hassle and so misunderstood until the benefit is seen. Some detours occur in our personal lives rather than a literal road but they are there for much of the same reasons. Life detours redirect us from danger, misfortune or even toward something better even if we don't see it at the time. I recognize little road blocks in my life all the time. Such as a car in front of me driving slower than I want to go. This is when God says, "This is to slow you down and protect you from yourself". How about a job opportunity that you just know was meant for you but at the last minute, falls through the cracks? And I know we've all had thoughts or opinions that may not be the most positive but before we go too far in acting on them something happens to reveal a truth about the matter that changes our perspective.

Again, that is God protecting us from ourselves, our narrow vision of the world and of others.

One of the most intriguing detours of life I have ever known was that of the apostle Paul in the Bible. Paul started out as Saul, not a disciple but a persecutor of members of the early church. Saul first appeared in the presence of the disciples during the stoning of Stephen. The disciple Stephen was preaching to the Sanhedrin and speaking of their sin. The people who heard his words were infuriated and wanted him dead. They began to stone him and those who witnessed it pulled off their coats and laid them at Saul's feet. Saul gladly stood watch over their coats in approval of their actions and the death of a disciple. He saw this event as furthering his purpose to put an end to the Way, which was the early church (Acts chapter 7).

After this, Saul went to the high priest to appeal to his dislike of those who claimed faith in Jesus Christ. Saul asked that he be given letters written to the synagogues in Damascus stating that if he found anyone of the Way he could arrest them. As Saul approached Damascus traveling the Damascus Road he came to a detour. Suddenly a flash of light surrounded him and he fell to the ground. Then he heard a voice say, "Saul, Saul, why do you persecute me?" Saul immediately asked who was speaking to which the voice replied, "I am Jesus whom you are persecuting" (Acts 9:4-5). Then the voice told him to get up and go into the city until he received further instructions. This was easier said than done because when he got up and opened his eyes, he realized he was completely blind. He remained blind for three days. Fortunately there were men with him who led him all the way. Talk about an unexpected change of plans! This is not at all what Saul had in mind but it is exactly what he needed for drastic change to occur in his life. This drastic change would positively effect the people of his day as well as generations to come (Acts 9:7-9). While in Damascus, Saul prayed and awaited what might happen next. At the same time, a man named Ananias saw a vision that told him where Saul was and that he was to go to him. He was very concerned of Saul's reputation for persecution and his intent to arrest those claiming faith in Jesus. God gave assurance that this was his will and Ananias went to Saul. When he entered the house where Saul was staying he put his hands on him and told him of all the Lord had said. He told him that he knew of the encounter he had on the road to Damascus and that God had sent him to Saul to restore his sight and give to him the gift of the Holy Spirit. Immediately, scales fell from his eyes, he began to see and he was baptized. From that time on Saul was preaching in the synagogues of his experience and revelation that Jesus is the Son of God (Acts 9:10-22).

The life altering experience that Saul had on the Damascus Road was definitely a life detour-a detour that changed his life and led the way to an extraordinary ministry. God even changed his name to Paul giving him a new name to go with his new life. With this new life he taught the way of redemption to those who would have not heard it otherwise-the Gentiles. To put it into other words, anyone who wasn't a Jew. This meant that now the gospel of truly living could be shared with the whole world. Paul definitely did his part in sharing that gospel and it all began with a detour on the Damascus Road. Sometimes detours are God's way of getting us on the right track-the path of his will. So the next time you are faced with a detour, instead of getting frustrated, take a moment to ask God, "Is there something you want me to do or change here?" It might just be the roadblock that changes your life!

Acts chapter 7 ____

Acts 9:4-5 ____

Acts 9:7-9 ____

Acts 9:10-22 ____

ADDITIONAL NOTES

10

Childish Adoration

I LOVE TELEVISION commercials almost as much or more than the shows that feature them. I think it's a toss up as to which type I like more; the ones that make you laugh out loud or the ones that are like a living Hallmark card that leave you reaching for the tissues before their sixty second sales pitch is finished. Recently, I saw one of a man walking through his home. The camera only allowed a view of him from the waist up but by his gait it was apparent that he had a limp, which caused movement to be somewhat difficult for him. This scene, which obviously was meant to evoke strong emotion, led me to feel sympathy for the man. That is, until the camera finally panned down to his feet where the cause of his affliction was made evident by the vision of two children approximately 4 or 5 years old attaching themselves as if by Velcro to each leg! "Oh, how cute!" I thought. The best images seem to be the ones that relate the closest to real life and having your kids constantly under your feet (or attached to them) is definitely real life!

Every parent has experienced the 'jungle gym' syndrome. This is when children are still at the age that they want to be as close to mom and dad as possible and the closer the better. This means arms and legs of parents make good substitutes for rope swings! The question every parent asks during this stage is, "Why?" The answer is love. A deeply, innocent and uninhibited love for that parent and the security they feel in knowing that love is returned in an atmosphere of safety, wisdom and protection.

When you think about it, this is the kind of relationship that is described in the Bible between the Lord and his children. He promises to give love, guidance and a secure future in him. He has given the ultimate sacrifice in his son to make sure we have everything we need-just like a good Father! The Bible says, "If your child asks for bread would you give him a stone? If he asks for a fish would you give him a snake? Would you give him a scorpion when he asked for an egg (Luke 11:9-10)?" To any one of those we would all say, "Of course not!" The Bible goes on to say, "If you know how to give good things to your children, then how much more is your heavenly Father willing and able to give good gifts to his children (Luke 11:13)!"

If we would really allow ourselves to meditate on that concept we would not be able to resist wanting to run to him and hold onto him for dear life! Dear life indeed! What a life we all could have giving honor to the one who created all, has power over all and wants nothing but the best for us; not just here but in our future home that he is still preparing for us!

Our future home is where we will spend eternity and have just as much time to show our love and gratitude for all he has done. Have you thought of how you will personally express your appreciation? Will it be by dancing like David did, or maybe you want to out sing the angels, or possibly you'll feel compelled to reverently and humbly bow before him. I don't think any of us will truly know what our reaction will be until we get there but if you have an imagination like mine, I'm sure you have anxiously tried to paint a picture of that wonderful day. I constantly try to conjure up the images in my minds eye of the day we all joyfully anticipate. These images include singing, dancing, bowing and reverence to the Lord by everyone around. As for me, I'm not taking part-at least not immediately. Why? Oh, don't misunderstand. I definitely see myself there-getting as close as possible to my Father and wrapped like Velcro to my Lord's nail scared ankle!

Luke 11:9-10

Luke 11:13

ADDITIONAL NOTES

11

Protected

WE ALL DO it; dream that is. If you're like me, by the time you are fully awake to recall a dream, it has vanished like a puff of smoke. Only a small handful of these nocturnal 'mini-epics' have I been able to retain in vivid detail. I believe God uses dreams to speak to us at times to avoid the distraction of our conscious minds and allow us to retrieve these images as well as the messages they convey. In them, he can teach life lessons, relieve fears, reveal future events if necessary or even give direction and purpose for ones life.

I remember one such dream. At the time, even though I didn't realize the significance of its message until many weeks later, when I woke that morning, I definitely knew there was one! What was the dream you ask? Well, I was alone at home and all was quite and calm. Then, I heard a very loud 'train-like' roar that seemed to engulf the entire house. Without thought, I immediately went to the garage and raised the door to witness a huge black cloud that was violently ripping apart everything in its path. With its twisting and turning, it gained strength as it continued to approach my home. Considering the obvious danger this scene presented, it would seem logical at this point to panic and run for whatever shelter I could find. Yet, that was not the case. Instead, I stood unmoved in an indescribable state of calm watching the storm as it devoured everything in sight and continued to draw closer. Then, as if on cue, the violently spinning black mass stopped its progression at the edge of the yard and tracked its course very precisely along the borders of my property without touching even one blade of grass. The raging dark cloud retraced its path, disintegrated into a vapor and then disappeared as if it never existed. The devastation it left proved otherwise. Mine was the only residence that remained untouched by the destruction. When I awoke from this graphic display, I retained a sense of peace along with wonder and intrigue for its possible message. For some time, I continued to ponder on the significance of the dream I was given.

Several days passed before God gave confirmation of his message. I was having a conversation with a friend as she said, seemingly out of the blue, "God will help you stand and give a sense of calm in the eye of the storm". I hadn't yet spoken to her of the dream, therefore she had no way to know how God was using her words to provide evidence of his personal message to me only days earlier.

Hearing this, I realized that God was preparing me for trials I would soon face and to remind me that through them all-he would never leave me. This message was presented by the specific images the dream entailed. The vision of a storm is intended to signify turmoil, unrest or even warfare in a person's life. A peaceful, calming presence always represents its source, which is God. The Bible tells of how Jesus was with the disciples while being caught out at sea in the middle of a fierce storm that they were sure would be the death of them. Jesus calmed the sea and allayed fears as he halted the storm by speaking, "Peace, be still (Luke 8:24)." In that moment, he not only subdued the torrential weather he and his disciples faced but also the scourge of doubt and uncertainty that plagued the hearts and minds of his beloved companions (Luke 8:22-25). By this gesture, he proved to them that their protection and security was not in their own physical abilities but in their faith in him. They didn't see how the storm began or how it could possibly be stopped but he did.

The same is true for us. We have no way of knowing what causes some things to happen as they do. In just the same way, we can not predict how certain things will turn out because we don't have the ability to see the future or the 'big picture' as they say, the way God does. He created all so it would stand to reason that he would understand and be able to control all for our benefit. Romans 8:28 says, "God will bring all things together for the good of them that love the Lord and are called according to his purpose". When we realize how much more he knows and can control if we just let him, not to mention how willing he is to provide for us in abundance, doesn't it seem logical and even practical to put our faith in the Lord instead of our own limited resources?

Maybe, because God knows us better than we know ourselves, he realizes our struggle to let go of our own control enough to let him work in our lives. This may explain why he uses things that catch us off guard, such as dreams, to get our attention and remind us of the ability we have in him to receive a fruitful, fulfilling life with guidance, security and protection beyond what our human minds can imagine. His enduring creativity in teaching never ceases to amaze me! How many ways he finds to bless His children-even in a late night movie of the mind!

Luke 8:22-25 ____

Romans 8:28 ____

ADDITIONAL NOTES

12

DAVID DANCED!

DURING ONE OF my nursing rounds, I went to check on one of my patients who had an IV antibiotic infusing. I realized the antibiotic was finished so I proceeded to disconnect the IV as I said, "Now you will be able to move around the room a little easier without having to drag around this IV pole." A visitor that was present in the room at the time said with a laugh, "You can even get up and dance a jig!" to which he immediately responded, "Oh no, God would get me for that!" As I listened I quickly debated over whether to respond to what I had heard or to just act as if I didn't. It only took a few seconds before I came to a decision as I heard myself say, "Well, David danced!" That comment provoked a look of wonder from the man. Then, to elaborate on my previous remark I said, "You know, king David in the Bible". The man abruptly turned to me with the strangest look of awe in his eyes and a slight grin on his face. He didn't even speak for several seconds but just gazed at me as if pleasantly confused. I couldn't help but giggle a bit as I looked at him and said, "Oh, you didn't think I would know that, did you?" To this remark, his grin progressed into a huge smile as a discussion of celebrating God's grace developed among those of us in the room.

As we talked, the demeanor of the man lightened and I began to think to myself that in this moment we were experiencing evidence of God's word. The Word states that where two or three are present in his name, there he will be also (Matthew 18:20). He revealed his presence in that room that day by the glow of the faces and the lifting of mood all around. All this brought about merely by sharing God's given knowledge of him to someone else.

Later that day, I took some time to really think of that brief conversation about how a man many years ago chose to glorify and celebrate God by dancing. 2 Samuel 6:13-15 says when the ark of God was returned that David uncovered himself, leaped and danced with all his might before the Lord. Scripture describes how he not only danced by baring his body but his soul as well, regardless of who saw, but later described his actions as being for God and God only. David expressed a desire to honor God further by even more humiliating behavior than that, if necessary (2 Samuel 6:21-22). No wonder David was noted as being a man after God's own heart (1 Samuel 13:13-14)!

How much more abundantly we could live and how much closer to God we would be if we fully understood the power in praising him with complete unrestraint. Our lack of understanding is not from God's lack of teaching I assure you! At least in my case, I know for a fact that I continue to live through lessons on this topic-some are the same lessons presented time and time again. When this realization comes, the enduring love and endless patience of God is revealed and the emotion of it is overwhelming at times.

The flood of emotion in itself is a blessing because the love that initiates it comes from the Almighty and engulfs us with warmth, security and the guarantee he himself has given us that declares we are his and he is ours. He is mine. I love to claim him and announce I am his. Those proclamations possess extreme power for they are the very reasons we were created. To praise, worship, love, honor, follow, obey and commune with him. When we do these things we gain strength and power in our lives to live as He wants-free and righteous!

To understand the meaning of life or to find ones purpose has become the ultimate goal of our society. The key that seems to be missing is the acknowledgment that we all were created for worship and praise first and foremost (Isaiah 43:7). The problem with accepting that fact seems to be that we still want purpose that is of ourselves. The struggle is in not realizing that a personal, individual, God given pathway for life is secondary. The one true reason for existing, in anyone's case, is to give praise to God. If we all could fully engage ourselves in that concept, the secondary purposes in our lives would be easier seen as God reveals them to us.

When you really think about it, praise is our reason for being -period. When we praise God, we unlock power in the atmosphere. That power affects others and draws them to him; possibly causing them to praise him. We know there is power in numbers and there is always power in the presence of the Lord. God says in his word, "Where there are two or three, there I will be also (Matthew 18:20)".

David must have had the right idea. Although, I'm sure in his day, a man who acted in such a way would have been considered a lunatic. He knew what pleased God and was not ashamed to give praise with total abandon. Because he did, God smiled on him, made him king, prospered him and called him a man after his own heart (1 Samuel 13:13-14).

What an example David has given to us all! In the story of his life we see a real man giving real worship and praise and receiving real blessing. We also see a man actually able to obtain the utmost of achievements-a close relationship with God.

So, thanks to a boy who became king so many years ago, I now know the power of praising regardless of appearances. Being blessed with this knowledge, I want more than ever to be a woman after God's own heart!

Matthew 18:20 ______________________________

2 Samuel 6:13-15 ______________________________

2 Samuel 6:21-22 ______________________________

1 Samuel 13:13-14 ______________________________

Isaiah 43:7 ____________________

Matthew 18:20 ____________________

1 Samuel 13:13-14 ____________________

ADDITIONAL NOTES

13

What's the difference?

What's the difference from one day to the next?

What's the difference whether it rains or shines?

What's the difference if I make this choice or that?

What's the difference whether I go to church this morning or sleep in?

What's the difference whether I speak against the wrong I see or just blend into the crowd?

What's the difference if I study God's word, hurriedly read a few verses or don't read at all?

What's the difference whether I pray continually for God's will or just when it suits me?

What's the difference? The difference is peace, hope, joy and love. These are just a few of the things that can make all the difference- things given through God's grace which he freely gives to all who are willing to receive.

What's the difference? Christ, he came to give us life.

What's the difference? The difference is between existing and living. According to Webster's definition, existing is merely being present whereas living is experiencing active operation. 'Christ came that we might have life and have it more abundantly' (active operation).

What's the difference? Do you live to exist or live for abundance?

What's the difference? He is!

JOURNALING PAGE

14

God Ordained Friendship

THE FRIENDSHIP THAT exists between those brought together by God is truly a miracle. Many people in this world do not understand such a bond. To anyone who has not seen it or experienced it for him or herself, the temptation to claim that it isn't real would be hard to resist. Those of us who have received the grace of God to be blessed with such a friendship know how real it is. Relationships that are ordained by God with his guidance and strength are true blessings that enrich our lives.

Recently I have been studying the story of David in the Bible. I have been enthralled by the story of David and Jonathan because of their special bond. The Bible says in 1 Samuel 18:1, "...the soul of Jonathan was knit to the soul of David, and Jonathan loved him as his own soul (NKJV)". God worked through this friendship to position David to be king and carry out his will for the benefit of his people. Both realized that their friendship was a God given bond and part of a larger plan for the fulfillment of the Lord's will. Considering all the obstacles that faced this relationship, expressly the murderous attempts of the current king on David's life (which happened to be Jonathan's father) the only explanation for how this close bond was forged and how it flourished was that it was God ordained.

Noticing this divine intervention in both their lives, each realized the impact of this special gift from God. This is expressed in the words of Jonathan when he said, "Go in peace! The two of us have vowed friendship in God's name, saying God will be the bond between you and me and between my children and your children forever (1 Samuel 20:42, The Message)! They both understood the strength gained by two people coming into agreement with God as the Bible says, "a strand of three is not easily broken (Ecclesiastes 4:12)".

God uses friendship to minister to us. Through these relationships we learn how to share more, love deeper, live larger and strive harder for a heart like his. The God ordained friendship is truly exemplified in 2 Samuel when David said that Jonathan was like a brother. He goes on to say in 1 Samuel, "Your love for me was wonderful, more wonderful than that of a woman." This is the kind of connection that few are blessed with and many don't understand because it is based on a Godly affection, separate from the carnal emotions and worldly views of today's society, which attempts to pervert what God has created. I know what a blessing and honor it is to have such a precious gift from God and I pray to never take it for granted.

My prayer is that my friends and loved ones are in God's will, protection and provision and that they know how truly loved and appreciated they are!

1 Samuel 18:1 ______________________________

1 Samuel 20:42______________________________

Ecclesiastes 4:12 ______________________________

ADDITIONAL NOTES

15

Rebel

IN THE 1950's we had Johnny (James Dean) who played the "Rebel Without a Cause", the teen who rebelled against authority. Then we had Johnny Yuma the lone cowboy who roamed the western countryside rebelling against the injustice he saw. Now in the present era we have Clint Eastwood who went against the norm and made the phrase "make my day" famous.

Have you ever wondered why we love the rebel and secretly root for him to come out the winner in the end? A rebel is one who participates in a rebellion or refusal to accept standards set by authority. A rebel who wishes to change those standards for the better is known as a revolutionist. You know several rebels but how many revolutionists could you recall? Could you take a guess at who was the first? How about Jesus? Jesus? A rebel? Yes. Jesus was the first revolutionist. Remember, a revolutionist is a rebel that pushes for positive change. What better example than the one who challenged the "law men" of his time; the Pharisees.

Jesus was not against the law itself but rather the use of the law to confine, restrict and spiritually hinder those who attempted to live by it. Jesus explained in the Gospels that he did not come to destroy the law but to complete it. Romans 6:14-23 says, "for you are not under the law but grace". In other words, the ultimate goal for all is to honor and obey God as well as serve one another in love. If we constantly strive for this goal we can live by grace while reverencing the laws God intended.

One of the first rebellions of Jesus was recorded in the book of Matthew the 23rd chapter as he spoke to the Pharisees and teachers of the law. Instead of addressing them with the honor they were accustom to, he called them hypocrites! In verse 23 he says, "Woe to you, teachers of the law and Pharisees, you hypocrites! You give a tenth of your spices-mint, dill and cumin. But you have neglected the more important matters of the law-justice, mercy and faithfulness. You should have practiced the latter without neglecting the former". He called them hypocrites for their lack of compassion. In fact, throughout the New Testament He called them hypocrites six times and blind five times! How's that for rebelling against the establishment?

Jesus explained that righteousness was more than a set of 'black and white' rules to follow. It was more about matters of the heart than learning routines and rituals. In this explanation he made it clear by making the Pharisees examples as he said, "When you give to the needy, don't announce it with trumpets as the hypocrites do in the synagogues and in the streets to be honored by men. I tell you, they have received their reward. Rather give in secret so that the Father who sees in secret will reward you (Matt. 6:3-4)". You know the type. There's always one in the crowd that has to say, "Look at me and what I've done". It's rather annoying, isn't it? It's also not pleasing to God. Jesus expressed his disapproval for this behavior by stating, "Unless your righteousness surpasses that of the Pharisees and the teachers of the law, you will certainly not enter the kingdom of heaven (Matt. 5:20)". Wow! That's serious stuff! But then, when eternal futures are at stake it's time to get serious!

Jesus put into action his true rebellion when he did the unthinkable. He healed a man's hand on the Sabbath. Knowing that the Pharisees would jump at the chance to slander him and shake the faith of those who believed, he asked them a question. He asked them in Luke 6:9 what was lawful to do on the Sabbath-good or bad? Knowing that they couldn't deny healing someone would be an act of good, he left them speechless. Angrily but quietly the Pharisees merely watched as Jesus healed the man's withered hand. Oh, but this rebel was just getting started!

In the next chapter of Luke, a Pharisee named Simon invited Jesus to dinner. He went and as he was sitting at the table a woman living a sinful lifestyle known to all entered the room. Weeping, she knelt at Jesus feet. She washed his feet with her tears, dried them with her hair and anointed them with perfume. Simon thought that surely this proved that Jesus was not a prophet or he would have known what kind of woman this was and turned her away. Instead Jesus, knowing the thoughts of his host, told a parable of two men who owed money to a lender. One owed much the other owed little. Both pleaded with the lender and their debts were forgiven. Jesus asked Simon which of the men loved the lender more to which he replied, "The one with the larger debt". Jesus affirmed Simon's answer. He then reminded Simon that he did not give him water for his feet or a kiss as he entered the door, yet this woman had given him all this and more. Because of this great act of love, her debt of sin was forgiven. The Pharisees were appalled at his response! The only one in that room who understood the truth had just been given the most precious of gifts-forgiveness, grace and love of the Almighty!

When the Pharisees finally found a way to accuse Jesus they thought that they had won. When it led to his crucifixion they thought their honored positions were to be challenged no more. They did not know that the ultimate rebellion had yet to come! While on the cross at his last breath, the veil of the temple was torn from top to bottom. This was a message from God that the law had been fulfilled and was no longer the authority but Christ was. Three days after his death, when decomposition of his body had long taken over, Jesus rose from the dead! Then he appeared to his disciples-not just in spirit but in flesh and blood!

No other rebellion has ever been so revolutionary to change the world as well as hearts and lives as Jesus was and is. What's more, this revolution is as real today as it was during the days of the disciples! Want to make your mark on the world? Want to stand out from the crowd and be different? Go ahead, be a rebel. Just use Jesus as your role model.

Roman 6:14-23 ____

Matthew 23:23 ____

Matthew 6:3-4____

Matthew 5:20____

Luke 6:9 ____

ADDITIONAL NOTES

16

Independence Day

INDEPENDENCE DAY, OR 4th of July as most of us know it, is a time of celebration for the freedom our nation has earned and fought for. This precious independence was not intended to allow us to be able to say or do whatever we want. The efforts our forefathers put forth were for much more. In those days, England was very controlling of its citizens and freedom to live as one wanted was not an inherent right. Areas such as the right to live a prosperous life, worship as one believed as well as the right to refuse taxation without a reasonable purpose, were not accessible for the people of England. A small group not only felt the injustice from England's oppressive control but were ready and willing to do whatever necessary to fight for the changes needed to obtain freedom for themselves as well as generations to come.

In many ways, addiction can be just as controlling and just as oppressive. When a person has an addiction, that addiction takes control and hinders that person from pursuing any other goal in their life. Moving forward and creating a meaningful, productive life is only a fleeting dream when bound by addiction. In like manner as our founding fathers, a fight for positive change is the only answer to achieve freedom from the bondage.

Any hard fought win for freedom deserves celebration! That's why July 4th of every year is so important. But besides the picnics, barbecues and fireworks of the 4th of July, there is a different type of 'independence day'. A more personal event that takes place when a person makes the decision to break free from the control and oppression of addiction-a personal independence day. This day is not unlike the one we observe to recognize the victories won to make our nation one that can stand strong and on its own. To gain independence from addiction, a person must be willing to do whatever necessary to fight its control. Just as our forefathers used every resource available to succeed, it is necessary to use every means of support open to you.

The fight for independence is never easy. You will have to fight just as those who founded our nation had to fight, struggle, face hardships and resist thoughts of failure. They faced many obstacles and setbacks but never gave up their vision for freedom. The road to freedom from addiction is traveled with many of the same pitfalls and conquered with the same determination-never give up! Independence: the first step to a better life!

JOURNALING PAGE

17

True Love In Deed!

"My little children let us not love in word, neither in tongue; but in deed and in truth." I John 3:18

THE NEWS IS full of horrific stories of parents mistreating and abusing their children all the while confessing deep love for them. Or a spouse acting in much the same way by physically beating the one they vowed to protect and honor while continually attempting to justify their actions as part of love. In situations such as these, it is hard for most of us to see the love that is professed by the behavior witnessed. On occasion, though sadly not as often, we are privileged to observe a physical reinforcement of proclaimed love by the consistent heartfelt gestures of the person making such claims. These are the claims we tend to believe most readily.

Whether we realize it or not, we determine much of what we believe not by what we hear but what we see. In the Bible, this point is clearly discussed in detail as Jesus explained how the visible fruit of a person's life reveals the true heart of that person. In Matthew 8:17-18,20 Jesus said, "Every good tree brings forth good fruit but a corrupt tree brings forth evil fruit. Wherefore by their fruits they shall be known." So it is that if we do not communicate with our actions the same message we speak with our mouths then our efforts are in vain. What is said carries little meaning if it is not reinforced with similar behavior.

The Lord knew how important this lesson was which is why it is found so often in many different forms throughout scripture. God continually tells us to love our neighbor, be thankful, be angry and sin not, be kind one to another, be tenderhearted and forgive one another as God has forgiven us. He knew that it wouldn't mean much if we professed the love of Christ but failed to let others see it in our lives. The Lord reaffirmed this message in the 13th chapter of 1 Corinthians, as the Holy Spirit led Paul to explain that charity is the greatest act of love we can present. Charity is described as long suffering and kind without being boastful or proud and is not easily provoked while taking joy in truth instead of evil. Paul goes on to say that the most enduring things in this life are faith, hope and charity but the most important is charity. Why would that be? Well, the definition of charity is the goodwill or love for humanity. If we first have sincere charity for others then faith and hope will be nurtured as a result.

The most perfect example of charity was Jesus. His love for humanity was made evident in the sacrifice he gave of his life as well as all the suffering he endured while making that sacrifice. Before this gift was given, he continually taught lessons of how to live a life of honest goodwill. As long as mankind has been in existence, we have questioned what is charity and who should we be charitable to? To finally answer that question without further doubt, Jesus gave us the parable of the Good Samaritan. In Luke chapter 10, Jesus responded to the query of what one should do to receive eternal life by commanding that we love God with all we have and our neighbor as ourselves. Knowing we humans tend to look for a 'loophole', he told the story of a traveler who becomes robbed, beaten and left for dead. Several supposedly respectable people who didn't want to get involved passed the man. The one who chose to show charity to the man by taking care of his needs was a Samaritan. Jesus used this tale to explain that we should all consider anyone in need as a neighbor and use the resources he has given us to provide for the needs of those whom he puts in our path.

To allow yourself to fulfill the needs of someone else, many different resources may be specified but one thing is required. That requirement is a servant's heart. Christ discussed many times throughout scripture of what a servants heart meant. During his life on earth, he was the ultimate example and taught us how, through servant-hood; charity can take root and grow in the human heart. The most memorable occasion ever told in the Bible was when Jesus set aside the status of leader to become servant to the disciples. he became their servant when he washed their feet during the last supper as an act of deeply, devoted love for them. By this humble act, the disciples too were humbled at the depth of love it expressed as well as the change it created in their hearts due to the sincerity it implied. What they saw in him and his life changed them forever.

When we meditate on the goodness of God and the charity Jesus showed to all he came in contact with, should we really have to question how the Lord wants us to live? The meaning of Christian is to be Christ-like, which means that to call ourselves Christians we must strive to be more and more like him everyday. Striving to be more like him requires continually being aware of our actions and what they say to others.

Do your actions speak love or loss; life or death? Do they reinforce what you speak with your mouth or are the two contradictory? Christ loved the world by his words as well as his actions. If we are to be like him, we must not just speak as though we love others but show them-for only then will they really start to believe. By showing love in our consistent goodwill toward others we are genuinely proclaiming the true love of Christ not just in word but in deed- true love indeed!

1 John 3:18 ______________________________

Matthew 8:17-18, 20 ______________________________

1 Corinthians 13______________________________

Luke 10______________________________

ADDITIONAL NOTES

18

Handful of Change

IT'S CHRISTMASTIME AND all the stores are adorn with festive lights and decorations in an attempt to enhance the holiday spirit. Bell-ringers faithfully stand by each storefront with their clinking bells, big red pots and "Merry Christmas" greetings hoping to acquire all the change left in the hands of those last minute shoppers. Many put the change in their pocket and walk on by without a second glance. Others drop the change into their pocket without a second thought, mainly to avoid the hassle of having to put it back in their wallets. 'After all it is just change, right? What difference could a few coins really make? It's not like a handful of change is going to make a difference in the world!' Yet, the truth is, a handful of 'change' could make a difference in someone's life without costing a penny!

Okay, so that last statement may sound like a riddle but it really isn't if you think about it. When someone speaks of a 'handful' or something 'in hand' they are usually referring to something in one's possession (Webster's Online Dictionary). Most possessions are considered valuable if only to the owner. Many things could be considered possessions but not all are monetary. Some possessions come in the form of skills, talents, abilities or even personality traits. Not everyone has great wealth or vast belongings within their grasp but everyone has something of value. Genesis

1:27 states that we are created in God's image and Thessalonians chapter 5 says "you are all sons of light and sons of day; we do not belong to the night or to the darkness" (v.5). Those of us who are of the day are to be "self-controlled, putting on faith and love as a breastplate and hope of salvation as a helmet" (v.8). Christ died for us so that whether awake or asleep, in a crowd or all alone, thinking the whole world is watching or thinking no one can see what we do, we should strive to "live together with him" (v.10). All this may make living for Christ seem like a very daunting task but the word continues to elaborate in this chapter of how we can achieve this. We are to comfort and edify each other, be at peace with one another, counsel the disobedient, console the faint-of-heart, encourage the weak and be patient! Whew! Sounds like a lot, huh? Then again there is a lot of change that needs to take place and a lot of people that need to see God's love. God chose to work through each of us by using the special traits he has given each of us to reach the hurts and needs of those around us.

God created us all to be individuals with gifts and abilities unique to each of us. 1Corinthians 12:4 says that each of us has gifts given by the Holy Spirit that are not always the same as someone else's but are just as important. These special traits are not meant solely to enrich our own lives but to help others. Jesus proved this point when he said that all the commandments "are summed up in this one rule; love your neighbor as yourself" (Romans 13:9). By using our gifts to help others as God intended we could see a positive 'change' in the lives of those around us! It doesn't take much to make a radical difference in someone's life but it does take compassion and a willingness to give of yourself.

Did you know that God not only desires that we use our abilities to help others but requires us to give of what we have so that others might be blessed also? Requires? How is that so, you may be asking. Yes, it's true that God loves a "cheerful giver" but that doesn't mean that any one of us can truly call ourselves Christians and yet say, "I just don't feel like it, or "I'm just not that kind of person", "Someone else will do it, I'm just not good enough" or what about, "I'm doing alright now but what if I fall on hard times later. No, I better just keep all I have for myself". None of these views are what God intended for his children and they certainly do not align themselves with scripture. Jesus makes this very clear in Luke 12:48 when he says that "from everyone who has been given much, much will be demanded and from the one who has been entrusted with much, much will be asked". Reading this makes it plain to see that God blesses each one of us with the intent of having those blessing shared with those around us. God is not selfish with us, and Jesus, our example, was not selfish with anyone he encountered. So, how can we justify being selfish with those things that have been given to us by God to edify others? It never has to be outrageous or grandiose, just whatever you have to give-given in love. 1Corinthians chapter 12 describes how each of us has been blessed with something to give. It doesn't matter whether your gift or ability is the same or different as someone else's. All that matters is that you use it to show God's love and realize that in doing so you will not only edify others but also honor God in the process!

It is true that the world seems to grow darker everyday and the nightly news broadcasts only one negative story after another. With all the pain and suffering being experienced in the world you may ask, "How can my small contribution ever amount to anything that would matter?" My response is, "Remember Jesus words when he said, if you have faith, you can move a mountain. Have faith that God gave you this ability to make a difference and if you share it as God intended, you will." How awesome to have such an active role in the kingdom of God! In Luke 13:18-19 Jesus compared the kingdom of God to a mustard seed planted in a garden. Even though it was so tiny that it seemed extremely insignificant, it is used anyway. From that mustard seed grew a tree, full enough to shelter the birds in its branches! He goes on to tell of a woman who mixed yeast into a large amount of flour until it worked through the entire lump of dough (v.20). In these stories, Jesus was explaining that what we have and see as 'nothing', God can use to change lives, further his kingdom and increase his glory! If you want to see a change you have to be the change. What God has placed in your hand is uniquely yours, a true gift to you and a blessing of hope to others. You could say that your God-given gift is your 'handful of change' for the world!

Genesis 1:27____

Thessalonians 5:5, 8, 10 ______________________________

1 Corinthian 12:4____________________________________

Romans 13:9____

Luke 12:48 ____

Luke 13:18-19, 20____________________________________

ADDITIONAL NOTES

19

Zoe

As I watch you run and play, I see what carefree looks like. I see how happiness can come from simple pleasures like the joy you find in rock collecting, the comfort you get in carrying around your favorite toy or the warmth of finding a patch of sun to nap in on a cold, February afternoon. In you I see how simple it is to find true joy in life when you show what it means to live, laugh and love.

Zoe is your name but love is the lesson you teach by example to all those around you. You live not wanting to miss a thing, going full throttle until sleep sneaks up on you. And you laugh-yes laugh! I am amazed that you can give such a peculiar, almost thoughtful look through those big, passionate brown eyes. After which, you throw your head back with a grin, take a running head start and tackle me a huge hug and a lot of love. How enlightened I feel when I allow myself to learn from your unpretentious, sincere and innocent nature.

Oh, how much richer our lives would be and how valued our loved ones would feel if we all followed your example of living life to its fullest and loving without hesitation. When we find such an impressive example of simplistically living with a pure heart, we are wise to follow it. Even wiser, to refuse to be hindered by the fact that this message of how to live a contented life is packaged in a four-legged, pug nosed bundle of fur!

Maybe you can't actually speak but you communicate volumes. Oh, the volumes you could teach us humans! If I could actually have a conversation with you, I would tell you how thankful I am for the insight you have given me. Maybe I'm the one who doesn't understand for somehow assuming that you don't already know. Zoe-your name means life. You definitely inspire life and give honor to your name!

JOURNALING PAGE

20

Keys

THROUGHOUT YOUR LIFETIME you will be presented with many important 'keys': keys to your first car, first home, success or even love. However, the most important keys that you will ever possess are the keys to salvation. If you have never made a personal decision to follow Jesus, the keys listed below will guide you through the steps to salvation. Following these steps is a short prayer that will lead you in accepting Jesus as your Savior.

<u>Keys to Salvation</u>

- Acknowledge that you are a sinner and ask for forgiveness and acceptance.

"For all have sinned and fall short of the glory of God." Romans 3:23

- Believe that Jesus is Lord and has forgiven you.

"They replied, Believe in the Lord Jesus, and you will be saved-you and your household." Acts 16:31

- Confess that Jesus is Lord of your life.

"That if you confess with your mouth, Jesus is Lord and believe in your heart that God raised him from the dead, you will be saved." Romans 10:9

Prayer

Dear Lord Jesus, I know that I am a sinner but the Bible tells me that you died on the cross that I may be saved. I am truly sorry for all my sins. Please forgive me. Right now, I am asking you to be my personal Lord and Savior. Forgive me, save me and cleanse me from all my sins and guide me in every area of my life so that I may live according to your will. Amen

After making a decision to follow Jesus Christ, it is important to find a local church to become a part of for support and continued growth. Here are website links that will help you in the search for a church near you.

http://www.christianchurchtoday.com/locator/

http://www.worshipquest.org/

http://www.forministry.com/profile/ChurchSearch.cfm

www.ingramcontent.com/pod-product-compliance
Ingram Content Group UK Ltd.
Pitfield, Milton Keynes, MK11 3LW, UK
UKHW020135250726
13967UKWH00002B/667

9 781425 184513